THIS WALKER BOOK
BELONGS TO:

_____

_____

_____

First published 1990 by Julia MacRae Books
Published 1993 by Walker Books Ltd
87 Vauxhall Walk, London SE11 5HJ

This edition published 2008

2 4 6 8 10 9 7 5 3 1

© 1990 A. E. T. Browne and Partners

This book has been set in Palatino

Printed in China

British Library Cataloguing in Publication Data:
a catalogue record for this book is available from the British Library

ISBN 978-1-4063-1339-0

www.walkerbooks.co.uk

CHANGES

Anthony Browne

WALKER BOOKS

AND SUBSIDIARIES

LONDON · BOSTON · SYDNEY · AUCKLAND

On Thursday morning
at a quarter past ten
Joseph Kaye
noticed something strange
about the kettle.

Everything else in the kitchen
was in its familiar place,
clean and tidy.
It even smelled the same as usual.

The house was quiet,
very quiet,
and Joseph's room
was just as he had left it.
And then
he saw the slipper.

That morning his father had gone
to fetch Joseph's mother.
Before leaving, he'd said
that things were going to change.

Was this what he had meant?

Or

this

?

Joseph didn't understand.

Perhaps things
would be all right outside.
At first they seemed to be.

Joseph didn't know what to do.
Maybe if he went for a ride…

...or looked over the wall?

Was everything
going to change?

Joseph went back
to his room,
closed the door,
and turned off the light.

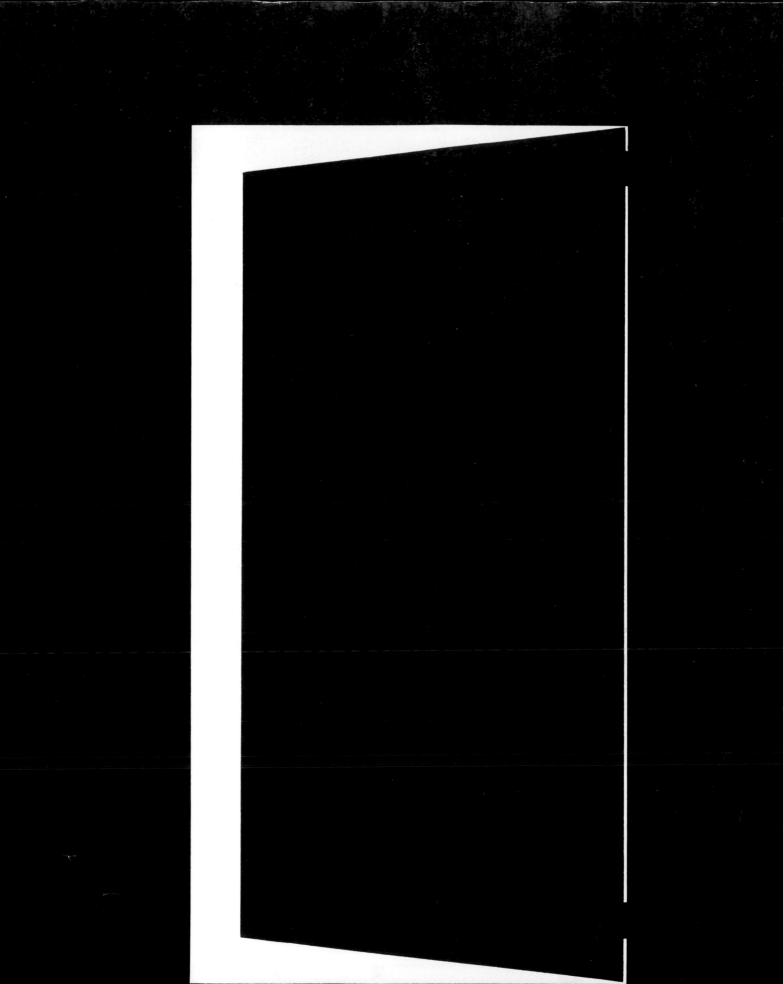

When the door opened,
light came in
and Joseph saw
his father,
his mother,
and
a baby.
"Hello, love," said Mum…

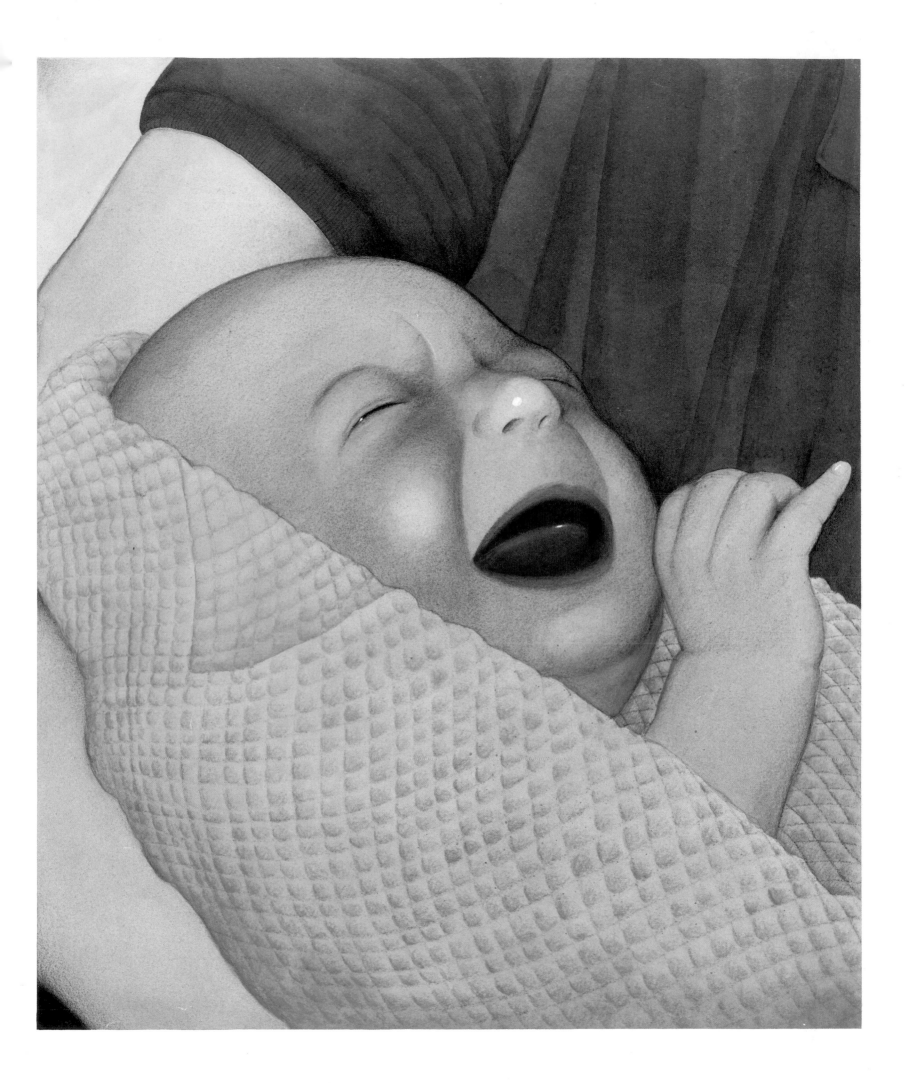

"…this is your sister."